The Captain, The Countess and Cobby the Swabby

"A Book about Honor"

Written by
Mary Hollingsworth

Illustrated by
Daniel J. Hochstatter

"On my *honor* I will try to do my duty to God and my country. . . ."

Marcy stopped saying the Girl Scout motto she was learning. "On my *honor*. I wonder what *honor* means? I know, I'll go ask Uncle Elzy. He knows everything."

Marcy found the retired sea captain in the study of his old house reading his big, worn Bible. She gave him a quick hug then plopped down on the rug to scratch the big tomcat. Captain Stash rolled over on his back and began to purr. He was named Stash because of the black moustache under his nose.

"Uncle Elzy, what does *honor* mean?" asked Marcy.

"*Honor*, eh?" Uncle Elzy took off his glasses. "Let's see, I remember an old sea story about honor."

"Will you tell it to me?" begged Marcy.

Uncle Elzy turned through his Bible and stopped. "It's a story a lot like the tale of Queen Esther in the Bible," he said.

"What happened?" asked Marcy, rubbing Captain Stash's fur the wrong way by mistake.

"Yeeeow!" squalled the cat and ran under Uncle Elzy's chair.

Uncle Elzy chuckled, "Well, here's the way I heard it. A countess and her people bought tickets on the ship of Old Patch the pirate and his crooked crew by mistake."

"Why was it a mistake?" asked Marcy.

"Shiver me timbers, Matey! Old Patch was about the meanest varmint on the high seas," he said seriously.

Uncle Elzy got up from his rocking chair and walked to the round window. He looked out through the brass telescope at the ships in Hargrave Harbor.

Then he said, "Old Patch's first mate was an evil bloke named Cobby the Swabby. Cobby thought he was really important. So, he tried to make everybody on board salute him."

"But the countess's cousin would not salute Cobby," said Uncle Elzy. "Cobby became so angry he decided to throw the countess and all her people overboard. Then he tricked Old Patch into signing an order to let him do it."

"Oh, no!" said Marcy. "What happened next?"

"The countess's cousin heard about Cobby's plan. He told the countess that she had to talk Patch into stopping the order. Well, that was the worst thing she could think of doing," said Uncle Elzy.

"Why?" asked Marcy.

"Old Patch was a pirate—a mean, cruel man," said Uncle Elzy as he sat back down. "Patch had threatened anyone who came to his quarters without being invited. He said he'd make them walk the plank!"

"What did the countess do?"

"At first she would not go. She was too scared. But she had too much *honor* to let her people down."

"*Honor!* There's my word," smiled Marcy. "Does it mean she was brave?"

"Yes, that's part of it," said Uncle Elzy.

Captain Stash crept out from under the chair and jumped into Uncle Elzy's lap.

"A countess's job is to protect her people," said Uncle Elzy, scratching Stash's ear. "She knew she had to go see Old Patch and do what was right."

"Even if he made her walk the plank?" asked Marcy with surprise.

"That's right. The countess and all her people prayed that God would protect her. Then she went below deck to Old Patch's quarters," said Uncle Elzy.

"She was as nervous as a sailor facing a great white whale. Suddenly, Old Patch's door flew open," whispered Uncle Elzy, "and Cobby the Swabby came out. He laughed at the countess as he went by. When Old Patch saw the countess, he stared hard at her," said Uncle Elzy. "She almost stopped breathing. Then he slowly motioned for her to come in."

"The countess went in and waited silently. Finally Old Patch smiled and said quietly, 'Come here and tell me what you need, Countess. I'll give you anything you want, even up to half of my ship.' You see, Matey, Old Patch had secretly fallen in love with the countess."

"Oh! That's great!" said Marcy.

"So, the countess told him about Cobby's evil plan to drown her and her people."

"What did Old Patch do then?" asked Marcy.

"He became so angry," said Uncle Elzy, "that he locked Cobby in the dark hold of the ship. At the next seaport he threw old Cobby off the ship. And he ordered his crew to protect the countess and her people."

"So," said Marcy, thinking hard, "honor means that you always try to do what's right, even when you're scared to do it?"

"That's it, Matey!" said Uncle Elzy smiling.

"And that's what I'm supposed to do as a Girl Scout," finished Marcy.

"Yes, and as a Christian," said Uncle Elzy.

"On my *honor* I will try to do my duty to God and my country. . . ." began Marcy on her way home.

Captain Stash stretched out in Uncle Elzy's lap and purred loudly. He approved.

"Some people live for God's glory, for honor, and for life that has no end. They live for those things by always continuing to do good. God will give life forever to them."

(Romans 2:7, The International Children's Bible)

If you would like to read more about honor you can read Esther's story in the Bible. (Esther 2:1-23; 5:1—7:10)